This edition is published by Armadillo, an imprint of Anness Publishing Ltd, Blaby Road, Wigston, Leicestershire LE18 4SE; info@anness.com

www.annesspublishing.com

If you like the images in this book and would like to investigate using them for publishing, promotions or advertising, please visit our website www.practicalpictures.com for more information.

Publisher: Joanna Lorenz
Produced by Nicola Baxter
Designer: Amanda Hawkes
Production designer: Amy Barton
Production controller: Steve Lang

PUBLISHER'S NOTE
The author and publishers have made every effort to ensure that this book is safe for its intended use, and cannot accept any legal responsibility or liability for any harm or injury arising from misuse.

Manufacturer: Anness Publishing Ltd, Blaby Road, Wigston, Leicestershire LE18 4SE, England
For Product Tracking go to: www.annesspublishing.com/tracking
Batch: 5510-22718-1127

Starting to read – no trouble!

This story of trouble underwater helps to make sharing books at home successful and enjoyable. The book can be used in several ways to help beginning readers gain confidence.

You could start by reading the illustrated words at the edge of each left-hand page with your child. Have fun trying to spot the same words in the story itself.

All the words on the right-hand pages have already been introduced on the facing page. Help your child to read these by pointing out words and groups of words already encountered.

Finally, all the illustrated words can be found at the end of the book. Enjoy checking all the words that you can now both read!

Trouble
under the
Ocean

Written by Nicola Baxter · Illustrated by Geoff Ball

ARMADILLO

Fred

Anna

fish

treasure

Fred and Anna are getting ready to dive.

"I want to see lots of fish," says Anna.

"I want to see lots of treasure," says Fred.

It is time to dive.

Ready, steady...
Splash!

Picture dictionary

Now you can read these words!

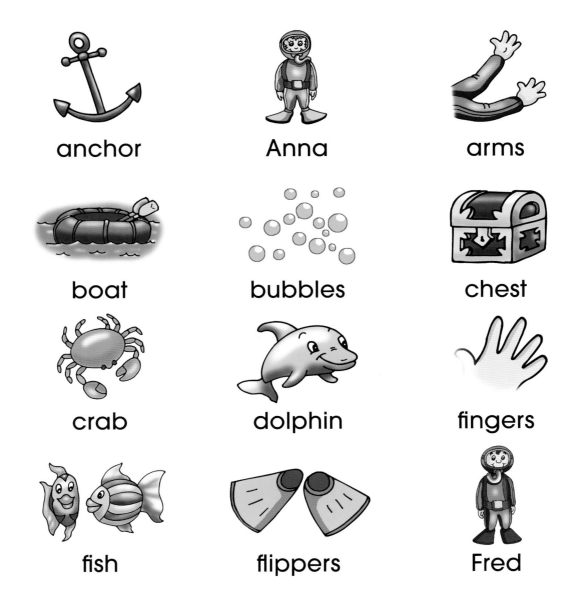

anchor

Anna

arms

boat

bubbles

chest

crab

dolphin

fingers

fish

flippers

Fred

Do you think Fred will find
some treasure?

boat

sun

island

map

"Thank you!" says Anna. She climbs into the boat.

"I saw lots of fish," she says. "And I saw some treasure! Do you want to dive again?"

But Fred shakes his head. "I think that octopus likes treasure, too," he says. "Let's stay in the sun."

Anna and Fred row over to an island. Fred begins to smile.

"Maybe there will be treasure here!" he says. "We must try to find a map!"

Fred and the dolphin help as
Anna swims up.

arms

lobster

snake

dolphin

Fred is swimming away from the shark. He sees lots of bubbles coming up. He swims down. There is the octopus!

Fred waves his two arms. The octopus waves its eight arms!

Some sea creatures try to help.

A lobster nips the octopus.

A sea snake tickles it.

A dolphin swishes past it.

At last the octopus swims away.

Now Anna is in big trouble.

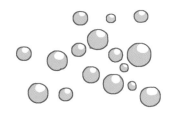

bubbles

starfish

shell

mask

Anna knows she is in trouble.
She tries to get free.
She makes lots of bubbles.

Now the octopus wants to be friendly. It gives Anna a starfish and a shell.

But Anna gives the octopus a big push.

Suddenly, the octopus grabs her mask!

The octopus is pulling her
to the sea bed.

sea bed

rocks

chest

octopus

Meanwhile, Anna is near the sea bed.

She sees something behind some rocks.

It's a chest full of treasure!

Then she feels something pulling her.

It isn't Fred.

It isn't funny.

It's an octopus!

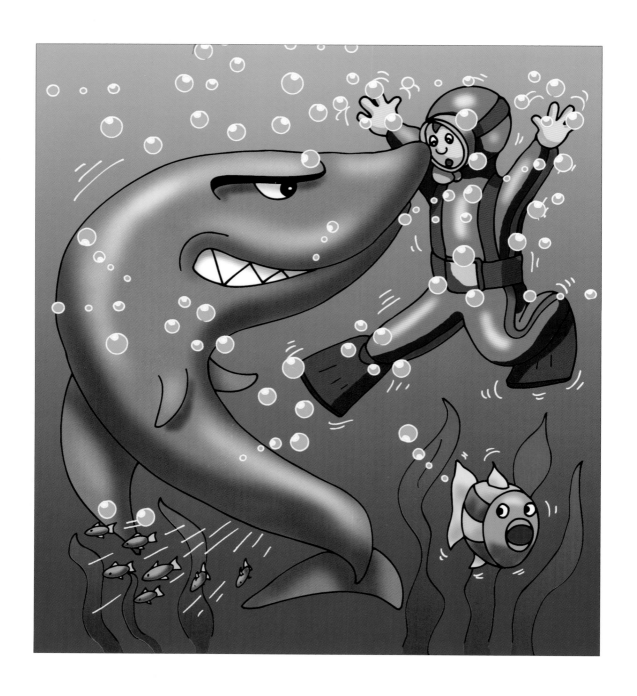

The shark has a very big nose!

wreck

crab

anchor

shark

Where is Anna?

Fred finds an old wreck.
What is inside?

There is no treasure.

There is no Anna.

But there is
a very big
crab.

Ouch!

As Fred swims away, he knocks
his knee on an anchor.

Ouch!

Then he comes
nose to nose
with a shark!

Oops!

Fred swims quickly away.

ocean

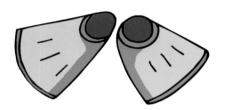

flippers

seaweed

fingers

Under the ocean, Fred and Anna cannot talk.

Anna is happy.

She sees lots of fish.

She flaps her flippers and swims quickly away after them.

Fred is not happy.

He tries hard to find some treasure.

But there is only seaweed … and lots of fish.

Ouch! A fish nibbles his fingers!

Splash! Fred and Anna dive!

island

lobster

map

mask

octopus

rocks

sea bed

seaweed

shark

shell

snake

starfish

sun

treasure

wreck